DUST STORM

BY **Jane McKellips**

PAINTINGS BY **Christopher Nick**

EDITED BY **Gini Moore Campbell**

OKLAHOMA HALL *of* FAME
OKLAHOMA HERITAGE ASSOCIATION PUBLISHING

OKLAHOMA HALL *of* FAME

Printed in Canada

ISBN: 978-1-938923-25-8
Library of Congress Control Number: 2016938012

DESIGN: SKIP MCKINSTRY

DEDICATION

This book is lovingly dedicated to
my Great Aunt Clara Dreyer who lived
in northern Oklahoma almost all her life,
survived through the Dust Bowl era,
and who contracted polio as a child.

Squeak...squeak. The windmill blades pinwheeled in the gentle breeze.

Clara closed her eyes and felt the warm sun on her cheeks. It was a bluebird spring morning, not a cloud in the sky. Too beautiful a day to stay indoors.

5

She limped her way across the yard. At the corral, a few barn swallows swooped overhead, chirping. "C'mere Sadie," cooed Clara, sneaking a carrot out of her pocket.

The mare pranced toward Clara.

"Clara! No!" Her papa rushed out of the barn. "I've told you to stay away from that horse!"

Clara jumped at hearing his command. She put the carrot back in her pocket, leaned on her crutches, and sighed.

"That horse could crush you in a second. Go on back in the house."

"But Papa..."

"Go on, now. You hear?"

Clara swayed across the yard, her crutches leaving little holes in the dirt. Her feet drew wavy lines where they swung along. For the last three weeks, she had snuck out to the corral and trained Sadie to eat a carrot out of her hand. Clara knew Sadie would never harm her.

9

The horse was a bright spot in Clara's narrow world. Polio had left her legs weak and withered at age four. She now wore braces surrounding her legs just to stand up and had crutches to help her move about. She had become used to them.

But her papa had not. He would not allow her to leave the farm. That meant no school, no trips to town, and no outings to see neighbors. Clara thought he was ashamed of her.

She let the house door slam behind her as she went inside.

Her mama was changing baby Sam's diaper in the bedroom. She had on her good dress, which meant only one thing.

"You goin' to town, Mama?"

Her mama nodded. "Right after Papa finishes the chores."

Clara wished she could go, too. She wanted to look at the fancy clothes in store windows. She wanted to watch people walk on the Guymon sidewalks. She longed to see and speak to friends and neighbors.

"I don't suppose..." began Clara.

Mama shook her head. "No, I'm sorry."

"But why? Why can't I go?"

"You know Papa's only trying to protect you. He thinks others will say or do cruel things and hurt your feelings. Many people think we must have done something bad and your polio was our punishment. So if they see you with us, they'll be reminded that we're bad people, and they might not allow us into their stores."

"But I don't need protecting. I can handle that. I'll stay in the car," Clara argued.

Mama shook her head. "No, Clara, not today. I'm sorry." She raised Sam up and kissed his pudgy neck. "Billy can stay here with you."

Hurt, Clara went back outside. At least she would not be left home alone. Again.

She watched as Papa herded her younger sisters, Elizabeth and May, into their old car. Mama got in holding Sam on her lap. And off they went, plumes of dust billowing behind on the dirt road.

Billy headed straight for the barn.

"Come on, Clara. I know where
Daisy hid her kittens."

She followed her younger brother
to some hay bales.

"Look down there," he whispered.

Clara peeked between the
bales and grinned. Five kittens
mewed and tried to walk on
shaky legs. Daisy, their mama,
kept guard close by.

After petting the kittens for a while, a breeze swept into the barn. Clara heard birds squawking and went outside.

High above her head, flocks of crows flew south. Jackrabbits raced so fast across the field it looked like they were being chased by hungry coyotes.

Sadie whinnied in the corral, panicked.

Billy came up behind Clara and pointed to the chickens. "Look!"

All their chickens were rushing into the chicken coop, and the wind was starting to moan.

"What's going on?" whispered Billy.

Clara did not know, but she was determined to find out. She went around the barn so she could see toward the north, and gasped.

A long, pencil-thin black cloud rose across the horizon. It was something she had seen before and hoped she would never see again.

"Oh no! Another dust storm," she yelled. "Billy! Shut the chicken coop door. Then put Daisy and the kittens in a box and take them in the house. Hurry!"

Clara moved faster than she thought possible toward the corral. She had to get Sadie inside the barn before the storm hit. The horse could die from breathing in too much dust.

She reached the corral gate and pushed it open. She moved to the barn doorway. Giving one loud whistle, she waved the carrot in the air.

"Sadie, get in here! Now!"

The mare raced into the barn and gobbled up the carrot in Clara's hand.

"Good girl," said Clara. She tried to shut the heavy barn door, but it dragged on the ground. She had to push hard and hold on to her crutches at the same time. Precious time slipped away. Finally, the door shut with a thud and latched.

Clara glanced back at the dust storm. The black cloud had grown tall and thick and billowed across the fields like a massive tornado turned sideways. It howled angrily as it rolled closer and closer.

Clara rushed toward the house. Fifty feet to go. Her arms ached. But she forced the crutches to hurry, hurry. Forty feet. Thirty feet.

Clara had only twenty feet left when the storm hit. Dust stung her skin like poking needles. It was so thick she could not see her crutches. She squeezed her eyes shut, remembering the story of old Mr. Kraft who had gone blind when caught outside in the last dust storm.

The ferocious wind threw her down. Clara lay on the ground, trying to hold her breath. Her arm ached where she had fallen on it. She had never been so scared. But even with the storm's fury pummeling her, she knew she had to get inside soon or she could die. The house was straight ahead.

She would have to crawl the rest of the way.

Keeping her eyes shut, she dragged herself along, braces, crutches, and all. Inch by inch her hands felt their way until they hit something solid. The porch! She pulled herself up the two steps. Grabbing the doorknob with one hand and holding her crutches with the other, she stood up and turned the knob.

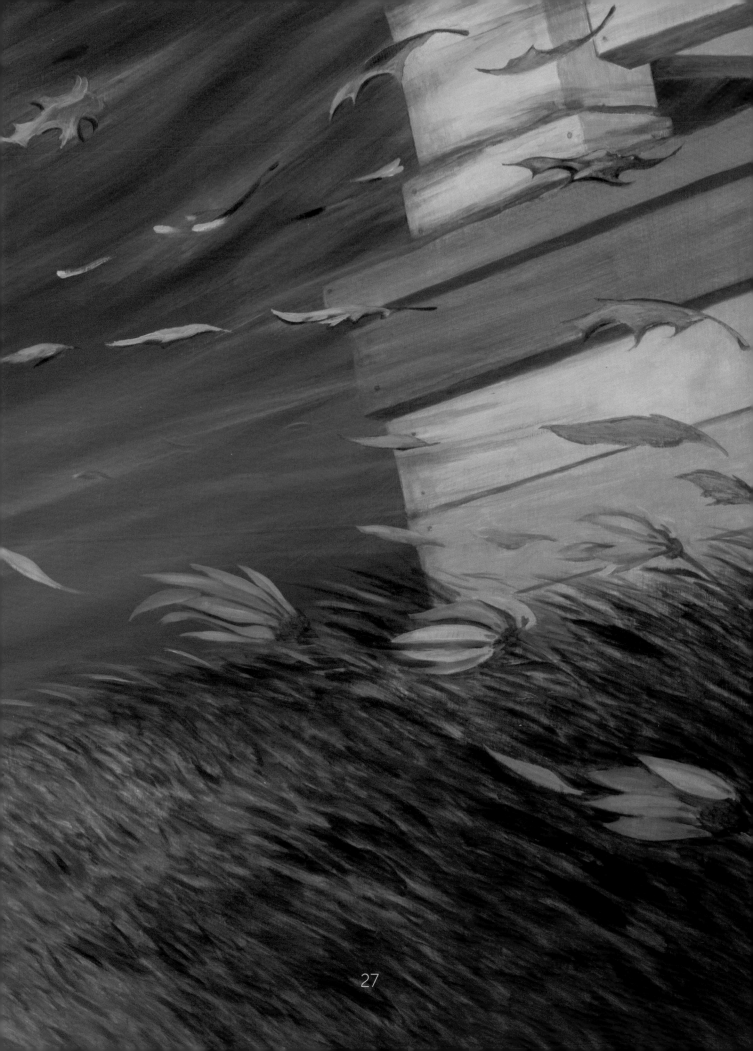

The door flew open, taking Clara with it. She fell to the wooden floor, bringing the storm inside with her.

She felt Billy's hands around her waist, helping her to stand. Then they both grabbed the door and forced it shut.

Clara bent over, coughing. Her mouth and nose were packed with dirt. Her eyes stung.

Billy patted her back. "Are you okay, Clara?"

She wiped her eyes with a wet cloth Billy brought her. Outside their kitchen window a shroud of blackness made it seem like night. Dust still blew into the house under the door and around the windows, whistling like a high-pitched scream. Clara grabbed a lantern and lit the wick to provide enough light to see.

"Go get some rags and towels," she told Billy in a hoarse voice.

After drinking a glass of water to clear dust out of her mouth, Clara ran water in the sink and soaked everything Billy brought her.

Then she and Billy stuffed the wet material into cracks around the windows and the outside door. That cut down on much of the dust blowing in, but not all.

Clara's heart skipped a beat as she saw the walls pulsing in and out like they were breathing. No living thing inside would stand a chance if the walls broke away.

Both she and Billy coughed in the dusty air. "Bring me the sheets off a bed," she told him.

Clara soaked them in the sink, too, and wrung out as much water as she could. Then she pulled a couple of kitchen chairs next to the couch and tented the sheets over them. "Bring Daisy and the kittens and crawl under here. The wet sheets will block out some of the dust."

Sitting on the couch with the lantern next to her, Clara took a sheet corner and wiped dust from her face. The cool dampness felt good against her stinging skin. She did the same for Billy. Daisy trembled with fear, but allowed Clara to wipe dust from her nose and the kittens' noses.

Finally, Clara could think of nothing else to do. Now they just had to wait out the storm under the sheet tent.

Sand crunched between her teeth. Her eyes felt swollen, and she could barely hear Billy's voice above the roaring wind. Outside, something crashed onto their porch, shaking the house.

Minute by minute, hour by hour, the storm raged on. Clara's muscles began to ache as she sat on the crowded couch. Total darkness enveloped them when the lantern ran out of kerosene.

Another crash. This time from inside, sounding like glass breaking. Clara hoped it was not the window near their tent.

Finally, the wind died down and its roaring stopped. Rays of light pierced the darkness. Clara raised the sheet and peered out. A haze of dust filled the air, making it still hard to breathe. She stood slowly, stretching to ease her cramping muscles. Clara's crutches crunched on broken glass from a fallen picture. She looked around and saw centipedes and other bugs crawling in the dust. "Eeuww." Clara realized they had crawled up from between the floorboards, probably trying to find clean air to breathe. She quickly sat down on the couch.

Billy grinned at her reaction.

"Mama's gonna hate this mess," said Clara.

Billy stepped over the bugs to open the kitchen door. "Clara, look!"

The outside no longer looked like her farm. It resembled a desert. Dust covered all Mama's flowers. Dust covered the rows of vegetables in their garden. Dust covered the young wheat stalks in the field. It looked like all the plants on the farm had been plowed under and tons and tons of dust poured on top.

The farm was cemetery quiet. Even the windmill was silent in the still air.

As she stood beside Billy, tears welled up in her eyes.

Then Clara heard a few cackles in the chicken coop and a snort coming from the barn.

"Sadie!" Clara grabbed a wet rag and struggled through deep dust mounds toward the barn. She inched the barn door open.

"C'mere Sadie," Clara said.

The horse stumbled forward. She sneezed and stood still as Clara wiped dust from her eyes, nose, and mouth. Clara brushed her coat until it shone. Sadie snorted and nodded her head as if to say thanks.

An hour later Clara cleaned the kitchen table and countertops while she worried about her parents and siblings. "They were probably in town when the storm hit."

Billy shoveled dust from the floor and threw it outside. "But what if they weren't? What if they were in the car?"

Clara bit her lip. They should have been back by now if they had found shelter.

Billy was the first to hear an engine. They looked out a window and saw a road grader pushing dust off the road. Her family's car followed close behind.

"They're here!" shouted Billy.

When the car reached their house, Billy ran straight into his mama's arms. Clara waited on the porch.

"Are you kids okay?" Mama asked, looking back and forth from Billy to Clara.

"Sure," said Clara, "just a little dusty."

"I'd better go check on Sadie," Papa said, ruffling Clara's hair.

"She's okay," said Billy, "thanks to Clara."

Papa looked confused. "Clara?"

"Clara put her in the barn," said Billy. "Then she closed the door. And after the storm, she wiped dust out of Sadie's eyes and nose, and she brushed Sadie's coat, and she..."

"Whoa," said Papa, scratching his head.

But Billy had to tell the whole story about how Clara saved Sadie, Daisy and her kittens, and Billy and herself.

By the time he finished, Papa was giving Clara a strange look. At first Clara thought he was mad at her for getting so close to Sadie.

"Come out to the corral with me," he told Clara.

When they got there, he put a foot on the bottom fence rail and watched Sadie eat oats from a dust-free trough.

"I suppose you cleaned out the trough, too," he said.

"I suppose I did," said Clara.

He was quiet for a long minute. "We didn't get all we needed in town before the dust storm hit, so we'll have to go back tomorrow. You want to come along?"

Clara smiled and stood up straighter.

"I suppose I do."

THE END

From left, Clara Dreyer (author's great aunt), Selma Dreyer (author's great-grandmother), Elizabeth Dreyer Burrill (author's great aunt), Warren Burrill (Elizabeth's husband), Opal Dreyer (author's grandmother), and Bill Dreyer (author's grandfather, Opal's husband, and Clara's brother).

AUTHOR'S NOTE

I have a deep connection with *Dust Storm*. All of my grandparents and great-grandparents who were alive during the Dust Bowl years lived on farms in northern Oklahoma. They told hair-raising stories about how they coped with the dangerous dust clouds. Sometimes they were trapped in cars on roads as the storms struck. But most of the time they were on their farms, huddled in their houses.

One fact they all said: there was no totally escaping the dust. It found its way into cars and homes around doors and windows. It came in between the planks of wooden walls. Often neighbors came down with "dust pneumonia" and were very sick, sometimes dying, from all the dust they breathed in. Luckily, none of my relatives died from it.

All the events in this book were based on stories I've heard from real people who lived through the terrible dust storms. Bugs really came up through floorboards, trying to find clean air to breathe. People who were outside and kept their eyes open during storms really went blind. Animals acted in the same way the story animals did when dust clouds drew near. After a storm finally ended, the outside to the horizon looked like a "black blizzard" had struck the region. Feet and feet of dust

blanketed everything, making the area unrecognizable.

I wanted to write this story in honor of my many relatives who lived through the Dust Bowl days in northern Oklahoma. Most of them continued to live on their farms, refusing to leave the land they loved. With neighbor helping neighbor, they weathered the drought and the storms, and "made do" until the 1930s decade was over and the rains came again.

I also had another connection with this story. My Great Aunt Clara Dreyer from northern Oklahoma was among the thousands of people who contracted polio before a vaccine finally eliminated it from the United States. As it did Clara in the story, polio left my aunt's legs weak and withered. She could only walk with the aid of crutches and leg braces. Clara was always very cheerful when I visited her. But she had a hard time moving about and didn't often leave her home.

FACTS ABOUT THE DUST BOWL

The 1930s was a time of drought and dust storms for people who lived on the American Great Plains. With little rain, crops withered in the fields. Poor farming practices left more and more topsoil exposed to harsh winds. Massive windstorms picked up the topsoil and carried it for thousands of miles. The hardest-hit states were Colorado, Kansas, Nebraska, New Mexico, Oklahoma, and Texas. Following the dust storm of April 14, 1935, known as Black Sunday, this area for the first time became known as "The Dust Bowl."

Farm families suffered the most. Without crops to sell and their animals dying from breathing in the dust, these families earned no money. By 1940 about one fourth of the people who lived in the Plains states had left their homes and moved away. That was about 2.5 million

The "Black Sunday" Dust Storm of April 14, 1935 overtaking Boise City.

It was not uncommon for families to abandon their homes following a dust storm.

people. Nearly 200,000 of these people ended up in California to start their lives over. They were not often greeted warmly. Many Californians did not want them living there. Californians called the Oklahomans who moved there "Okies." That's where the term Okie began.

The panhandles of Oklahoma and Texas have been characterized as the hardest hit regions. Guymon, the town Clara's family drove to for supplies in the story, is in the Oklahoma panhandle. In the farming community outside Boise City in the Oklahoma panhandle, 40% of the population moved away. Others stayed on their Oklahoma farms, living a meager existence. The long years of drought finally ended in 1939 when more rain began to fall.

FACTS ABOUT POLIO

Polio is an illness that is contagious. That means a person can get it from being around someone who already has it. In the worst cases people can become paralyzed, have trouble breathing, or die. It's been attacking people since ancient times.

Jonas Salk, head of the Virus Research Lab at the University of Pittsburgh, began his research on polio in 1947 and in April, 1955, the vaccine he developed became available for use in the United States. Today, there are reports of nations still affected by the disease.

In the 1930s there was still an unfair stigma attached to people with handicaps in the United States, such as those who had contracted polio. Society often thought an affliction was brought on by a lack of moral character or an inner weakness in those with handicaps or their families. These were the days before modern medicine could determine the real causes of some illnesses. People like my Great Aunt Clara Dreyer were often ostracized and kept away from normal society. They usually stayed close to home. If they walked down streets, neighbors might even cross to the other side of the street when they saw handicapped people coming toward them.

When the polio vaccine was developed, society finally understood that polio victims did not cause their own

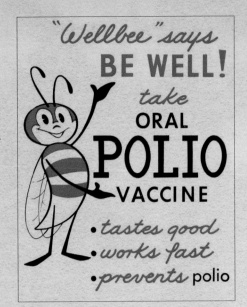
An early poster encouraging the prevention of polio following the development of an oral vaccine. Initially the vaccine consisted of a series of three injections.

illness. Then victims were usually treated with more kindness and respect.

One of the most poignant things I ever heard my Great Aunt Clara say when she became elderly was, "The happiest I've ever been is moving to this nursing home. For the first time in my life I'm surrounded by people and have someone to talk with all day long!"

Many times families were in transit when a dust storm hit, forced to ride out the storm in their car.